The Judge and the Prophet

Family Mantle

Tracy Henderson

Published by Tracy Henderson, 2023

THE JUDGE AND THE PROPHET

First edition. April 12, 2023.

Copyright © 2023 Tracy Henderson.

ISBN: 979-8215982518

Written by Tracy Henderson.

Table of Contents

I would like to dedicate this book to my two children Gabbrianna and Joseph Henderson. You guys bring me so much joy and love.

CHAPTER 1
THE NEW MISSION

It has been a month since Timmy died. Melissa, Tommy, and their mom were having a hard time coping. While they have good days, there are also bad days. Olivia and Gabbi spent many nights at Melissa's house listening to endless stories about Timmy. Gabbi loved hearing the stories, although Olivia sometimes gets tired of hearing them. It is during those times Gabbi sits Olivia down and talks to her. She tries to tell her to put herself in Melissa's shoes. Gabbi has to do this often. She is the type of person that does not like to hurt other people's feelings. Many times she bites her tongue while in the presence of someone so she does not say a hurtful word. Gabbi found herself doing this a lot while consoling Melissa. Maybe meekness is her weakness as Roger tells her.

On this particular night, Melissa told Gabbi a story of how Timmy felt when he got his new clothes the day before his death. It had been two years since he received any new clothes. Their dad always bought another woman's children clothes and toys and left his kids out. Melissa tried to hide how she felt about it, Timmy on the other hand was not good at hiding his feelings. She remembered the time their father bought a new bike for this woman's son on his birthday. Timmy had not had a new bike ever. He was riding a hand-me-down his father picked up at a yard sale. He paid five dollars down on the bike and did not pay the remaining balance. He still owed fifteen dollars on the bike, and as far as Melissa knew he never paid. Where did the money go you ask? Their dad not only had an affair with this woman, but he also had a gambling problem. He was a regular at the casino in the town they lived in. He had gambling debts he could not pay off. This caused him to turn to crime and other women.

To pay off one of his debts he sold Melissa's diamond necklace and matching earrings her grandmother gave her. They were not cheap pieces of jewelry. The appraisal value was well over five thousand dollars for the necklace, and two thousand dollars for the earrings. He walked into her room one night while she slept and stole them. He took them the next day to the pawn shop and sold them to pay the gambling debt. Since the jewelry was so pricey, he had money left over from paying the gambling debt, and that is how his mistress' son received a new bike.

When Timmy found out what his father did, he took a hammer to his used bike. He hit the bike so hard and so many times it was beyond repair. Timmy had a destructive temper before Jesus saved him. After he tore the bike up, he went into his mom and dad's room and took something his dad treasured above him, the picture he was hiding of the woman's son. His father did not realize Timmy watched him hide the picture, but Timmy witnessed him hiding it. Timmy busted the picture frame glass. Once the glass was broken, he took a black magic marker and colored all over the boy's face, and then put it back in the hiding spot. He left a note beside the picture that read, "I know about the woman and her boys. I know you bought her oldest boy a bike and I have a crappy one. I also know you stole Melissa's jewelry and now mom will know too." Timmy signed his name to it and drew a picture of a broken heart next to his name.

The day he received the clothes he pranced around the house like he won the lottery. He could not wait to show people the clothes. He meticulously placed each outfit on his bed and matched the shirts with the pants as if he was going away somewhere important. Little did anyone know he was. As his mother was picking out his clothes for school the next day, Timmy was set on a particular outfit. He picked out a red polo shirt with khaki pants. He chose red matching socks and the shiny penny loafers that came with the clothes. This would be the first and last outfit he would get to wear. He was buried in this outfit.

The story touched Gabbi tremendously. She laughed at the funny parts of the story but cried when Melissa told her about the clothes. Gabbi's brother Joseph was the same size as Timmy. Timmy's mother did not want to donate the clothes to Goodwill because she felt no one would appreciate the value attached to the clothes. It was not the dollar value she was worried about, it was the sentimental value attached to Timmy's wardrobe. The family decided to donate the clothes to Joseph. Gabbi's mom was grateful and cried as they gave Joseph a piece of Timmy. Now Timmy could live on as Joseph wore his clothes.

Joseph was not a typical child. He had some issues to deal with. For instance, he was always getting into trouble at school. This caused some stress in the family. He was pleasant to be around until he got mad. When he was mad it was Katy bar the door. He had frequent bouts with his temper at school, and that caused him to get put in detention, or worse, kicked out. Not only was Gabbi dealing with Melissa's family she was also trying to keep Joseph on the straight and narrow. This was a big task for an eight-year-old to tackle on her own. She needed help hugely. Every night before she went to sleep she knelt beside her bed and prayed for Melissa, Tommy, their mom, and Joseph. "Oh God, guide Joseph. Help him make the right choices in life. God, he is chosen by you. He is chosen to be a David for you. Help him fight against the evil forces not kids," Gabbi prayed every night. As tears rolled down her cheeks she would wail in intercession, "God save Joseph. Save Joseph." If you happened to pass by Gabbi's room as she interceded you could feel the heaviness she was praying under.

As she prayed she pictured Joseph being on that road Jesus showed her while she was in Heaven. The more she prayed the more images she received. She saw Joseph standing still sideways facing both directions. He scratched his head as he was trying to determine which road to take. When he was having a good day, she saw him on the path to Heaven. On his bad days, she watched helplessly as he walked the other path. She watched him walk with his heavy burden of wrong choices. She would wail as he fell beneath those bad choices. Suddenly an angel would rush up to him and help him to his feet. She watched as the angel consoled him before he was left alone again with his devices. "Oh God help him make the right choices. He needs you," Gabbi wailed. Sometimes she saw Joseph struggle as he turned it around. She would pray and watch as he began walking in the other direction. She could hear demons scream "No!" as he kept walking toward the right choice. "All the way Jesus. All the way," Gabbi would wail. The more she prayed the more he walked. Other times, she would not get to see if he turned to make the right choice because she would fall asleep from all the intercession she was making for him.

That night Jesus stood at the head of her bed. She felt him stroke her hair as she slept. "Come with me daughter," Jesus said. Immediately she was standing in a huge room. This room looked like something from another period. It looked like a Roman Collesium. The balcony was huge, and the seating started at the very top and went to the floor in a funnel shape. On the left side of this giant room sat all of the demons. On the right side of the room were not only the angels, but she saw Uncle Kenny, her grandmother, grandpa, and all the family members she met the first time in Heaven. There were two other family members she did not meet the first time that was in attendance. Her aunt Dianne and Uncle Steve aka Porky.

On the floor were two tables. Sitting on the left side was Satan. She recognized him because of a glance she got at him when Jesus allowed her to visit Hell. Satan was standing by the preacher that preached laughing and mocking him. Jesus and the Holy Ghost were at the table on the right. To Gabbi's surprise, she was also seated at the table with Jesus and the Holy Ghost. Where was she at? Jesus leaned over and whispered to her, "You are in the Court of Heaven. Watch and listen, I will explain it all to you later, " Jesus told her.

"This court is now in session," Gabriel answered. Seated on the bench was God the father. Gabbi had not been to the throne room yet so she only saw God at a glance the time Jesus showed her the mansions. " Gabbi you are now a member of the Court of Heaven. Jesus explains it to her sometime," God said. Jesus nodded his head in agreement.

As the court convened, Satan stood to his feet and approached the bench. He stood about a foot away from the bench and was trembling. You could tell he was intimidated standing in front of God. "What do you want Lucifer?" God asked him. "I want to talk about Joseph," Lucifer said. "What about him?" God asked. "You know your highness he makes bad choices. You know he cusses and gets in trouble at school. With your permission, I want to take him and sift him as wheat. I want to prove to you he will not serve you or your son," Lucifer said.

Jesus immediately stood up and objected. As he objected he held out his hands. The nail prints became illuminated. From the illumination, blood began to form and drip onto the defense table. "I am the reason Joseph will not turn against the trinity," Jesus said. "My blood covered all of his sins, but let's see what our newest member of the defense team has to say. Gabbi, you have the floor," Jesus said.

Gabbi stood up with great boldness. "Your honor, yes my brother makes bad choices. Yes, he cusses and throws fits, but that is no reason for Lucifer to get his dingy ratty hands on him. He will turn it around for you, I saw him do it in my prayers," Gabbi protested. "Denied," God said. Lucifer looked at Gabbi and told her," I will torment you and your brother until he gives in." As he talked, Jesus put his hand on Gabbi's head. Blood flowed from the top of her head and went down to her feet. "She's covered, Satan. Now you are excused," Jesus said. Satan and the whole courtroom disappeared leaving Jesus and Gabbi alone. "My father gave you a promotion Gabbi," Jesus said. He went on to tell her God was pleased with the way she helped Timmy's family deal with his death. God was pleased with the way she interceded for Joseph every night. "Deborah was a judge in Israel.

You are now able to sit on the council as a judge in the Court of Heaven. You are a spiritual judge. You have the right to judge sin, and whatever you judge it as that will it be. You are also a prophetess like Samuel was when he was a kid. You will know when to act as a judge and when to act as a prophet. At your words, Joseph will live his life because your voice carries weight here in the Court of Heaven. Intercede well for him. You are making a difference. You may not think you are, but for Lucifer to bring him before the Courts, he views Joseph as a threat to his kingdom. You will tear his kingdom down in Joseph's life as you intercede as a judge for him," Jesus said. Immediately Gabbi was back in her room sound asleep.

The next day Gabbi went to the cemetery to visit Timmy's grave. She wanted to see the tombstone they put on his grave. As she approached she noticed Jesus was sitting on the tombstone. She approached with curiosity. She was used to seeing him in her bedroom, now he was at the graveyard. Jesus looked at her with tenderness but she also knew he was there on assignment from the father. He was wearing a white robe with a bright yellow sash. He glowed about him that was beaming radiance. He was so beautiful to look upon.

"Gabbi I must share with you the role you will play for us," Jesus said. "My father ordained you to be a judge in the Court of Heaven. As a judge, you are given certain rights and powers. You have the power to bring a person's sins before my father in prayer and he will forgive them. You have the right to judge sin, and call it what it is. Just like you did for your brother Joseph in the courtroom, your plea will not go unnoticed. Satan recognized who you were in the courtroom. But your role goes deeper than that. Do you understand?" Jesus asked her. "I think so," Gabbi replied.

"As a judge, you bring judgment and order. You are also a prophet. This role brings judgment at times, order at times, and warns the person at times. Do you understand?" Jesus asked. "Yes, I understand, I hope," Gabbi replied. "Let me explain. This grave represents your brother's condition. He has some parts of him that are buried. He needs to be freed totally. He makes choices that are not right for him. As a prophet, you have the power to bring him out of his grave. There will be times you must act as the judge in his case. When he makes the wrong choice, you will be an actor in the Court of Heaven and cause judgment to pass from him. At the same time, you will act as the prophet and redirect him," Jesus said. "Now I understand," Gabbi said.

Jesus began to share with her the story of Deborah. She was the judge in Israel that whom God gave victory. He could have used anyone else, but Deborah was more worthy of the position. Anyone else could be used to help Joseph and others, but when Gabbi passed the test of humility with not only Olivia and Roger but Melissa, Tommy, and Timmy, she became the one God decided to use. She will judge between right and wrong. That was the purpose she was shown the path.

He also shared with her how Samuel became a prophet. She will be used to prophesy about situations and cause certain outcomes. Her brother needs a prophet to lead him in the right direction. Yes, he needs to be judged at times, but judgment without correction is useless and will not do him any good. "You must call Lazarus out of his grave Gabbi," Jesus said. Gabbi understood how Joseph was a dead man walking. He was alive physically, but in some areas of his spiritual life, he was dead. She must find a way to bring him back to life. She knew it was not going to be easy.

Jesus went on further and began to explain to Gabbi why Joseph was so special to him. He let her know he received the mantle that was intended for her brother JR. "JR was to have the spirit of David, but as you know God needed him in Heaven," Jesus said. "When someone in a family dies, the mantle or the spirit that was intended to be upon them lies dormant until someone else steps up and fills that place. Your dad could not fill that place. Your sister and oldest brother could not fill that place because they have other mantles and gifting that set them apart. Your older brother could not fill the place because he is a shaker. A shaker is not the same as a warrior prophet. Joseph was the one that inherited the mantle and the spirit of David," Jesus told her.

He let her know David was a special person in his eyes. He was not only a warrior, but he was a prophet. He became the king of Israel. His heart was so tender toward God, although he made stupid mistakes, that God had the prophet Samuel anoint him as king. David did not come from a good place as far as man was concerned. He was a shepherd boy. "Do you know what made a shepherd boy so special?" Jesus asked Gabbi. "No I don't," Gabbi replied. " A shepherd boy wrote some of the most inspiring Psalms in the Bible. He knew what he was talking about in the twenty-third Psalm when he said the Lord is my shepherd I shall not want. As a shepherd he had no one else in that field he could depend on. He had to depend on me. When he prayed he didn't just say words, he went into the secret place. He that dwell-eth in the secret place of the highest shall abide under the shadow of the Almighty, David wrote," Jesus replied.

It was because of his heart toward God that he became the king. Gabbi understood the role David played in the kingdom of God. Joseph was to fill that same role in his way. In himself, Joseph does not have any traits that scream king. He has issues that torment and keeps him bound. He has a heart that is second to none. He would give you the shirt off his back if he needed to. That trait can not be bought. When he loves he loves hard. There are not very many boys Gabbi knows that put their whole mind, soul, and body into it when they love someone. Joseph is that type of person. He is as unsettled as a young lion but has the heart of a king. That is what separated him from the pack. That has to be why God chose him to carry on where JR. left off. She wondered what JR. would have done with this mantle. "That is not for you to know daughter," Jesus said. "Oh, sorry Jesus, I was just thinking," "I know Gabbi, and I'm glad you were," Jesus said. "You are?" Gabbi asked. "Yes, because that lets me know you are putting a lot of thought into what I am telling you. This is a lot to grasp," Jesus said. "Uh yeah," Gabbi said. Jesus laughed when she said that. He always laughs when Gabbi says funny expressions. He loves her heart and her attitude. He wished all the people he worked with had the same attitude she does.

Before Jesus left her at Timmy's grave he showed her something that broke her heart. He flashed a scene of a broken road. On this broken road was construction equipment sitting on both sides of the broken road. There were no workers in sight to man the equipment. "I want to show you what Joseph is dealing with," Jesus said. "This is his mind. It functions, but it is broken in areas. It is your job to call the construction workers back to work," Jesus said. "How?" Gabbi asked. "This is where the mantle of the prophet comes in. When Ezekiel went into the bone-yard and saw the dry bones, he had to prophesy to the bones. Once he did that the bones came together. He then had to speak to the wind and breath was put back in them. The bones became an exceeding great army. As you prophesy to the construction workers I will bring them back to their post. His mind will be healed, but you must step up and prophecy," Jesus said as he disappeared. Gabbi knew she had great work ahead of her. Her brother was worth all the effort she had to put in. She wanted to see him get better, and she knew she held the key for that to happen. She can't let Joseph down. Failure is not an option.

CHAPTER 2
THE PRICE

The next morning around 3 A.M. Gabbi had a dream. In this dream, she was back in the Court of Heaven. She was standing at the very top of the Courtroom looking down. Standing beside her was Jesus. He had on a beautiful silk white robe and a purple sash draped over his right arm. He was holding a rose that he gave to Gabbi. She could read his mind as he told her, " I am the beautiful rose of Sharon. My beauty outweighs anything in the world. This rose signifies my beauty." She felt honored to receive the rose from Jesus. No one ever gave her a flower before, let alone a rose. "Why was she here though?" she wondered. Her thoughts and questions were going to be answered soon enough.

" Gabbi, Satan took notice of you the moment you came into the Court of Heaven yesterday. You are the youngest threat to his kingdom of this modern age. Nobody your age has ever been given access to the courts, yet here you are. Father wanted me to let you know you will see his face-to-face soon," Jesus said. This kind of frightened Gabbi. She was not ready to die and leave her family. She wanted to live, go to school, and be loved by family and friends. She didn't want to be buried six- feet under, not yet. "Jesus, I'm too young to die. I have too much living to do. True I would love to see my big brother again and not ever leave him, just not yet," Gabbi begged. "No, no, Gabbi. You misunderstood. When I said you would see father's face soon, I did not mean you were going to die physically. You are going to die, but not the way you think you are. You are going to go through a spiritual metamorphosis. The worldly things are going to die in you, and you are going to live for the things of God. When I said you would see father's face soon, I meant he was going to visit you himself. When that happens, you will be changed in ways you never dreamed," Jesus reassured her.

Gabbi stood there in her dream beside Jesus with great joy knowing she was not going to be like Timmy, at least not yet. She admired Timmy being with the Lord. He was not in any pain and was not suffering. She had so much left to accomplish, and she wanted to help her brother. How could she do that if she was dead?

They began to walk down the long flight of stairs of the courtroom. As they slowly walked she was able to take in all the beauty she missed the first time she was in there. The stairs and floor, although ancient looking, appeared to be brand new. They had a glimmer to them that allowed her to see her reflection. They were emerald in color. This was an emerald blue. She never saw an emerald blue before.

The walls were made of jasper. They were blue as well. She could not appreciate the beauty of the color blue until now. To her blue was blue. Now, she was looking at a blue never seen on earth. An amazing thing about the walls besides being so beautiful as they were singing to Jesus. As she went down the stairs the walls were singing Hallelujah. When she got to the bottom of the stairs the walls began singing Thou art worthy. Jesus seemed to enjoy the sound of the walls praising him. The more they sang the more he was enjoying himself. "The Word says "Let everything that hath breath praise the Lord. Praise ye the Lord," Jesus said. "I did not know the walls had breath," Gabbi said. "Gabbi, I want to explain to you about the imagination of God. When we made the heavens and the earth we made them out of nothing. My father loves to be adored. He adores far more than he is adored by humans. His countenance provokes praise. There is nothing we created, whether human, plant, or animal that does not draw from his countenance. The walls are no different here. They sing his praises, and mine as well because I redeemed mankind. A flower is not just a flower. A flower, even the rose I gave you is a vessel of praise. When I gave you that rose, it praised me," Jesus said.

"I get it," Gabbi said. She remembered the garden and the two trees. As her mind went back to that visitation Jesus told her, "Adam and Eve failed to praise me in everything they did and saw. They took them for granted their position, and was a prime candidate to lose their position. Never get to the place where you fail to recognize the significance of my father, myself, and the Holy Ghost. The moment you take it for granted, you will lose sight of it. When you lose sight of us, you lose sight of life itself," Jesus said. Gabbi put that advice to memory.

As they continued walking they approached the bench. "This is where God sits. It is called his throne," Jesus said. The throne was huge. She could put two of her, if not three into the throne. This was no ordinary seat. This seat glowed all around it. "This is the glory of the Lord," Jesus said. "The reason you or I cannot sit in his seat is that we can not take his glory. I possess glory but his glory is greater than mine. Sometimes I have to say as John did, he must increase but I must decrease. I do this out of respect for my father. See Gabbi I am the reigning king at this moment because I have not turned the kingdom over to him yet. When I come back for my church and sin is judged, not in the Courtroom, but in the throne room, then I will at that moment turn the kingdom back over to my father. Until then, he trusts me with it. This is the talent he gave me. If he gave some men this talent they would take it out and bury it. I took my talent out and put it to work. I brought souls into the kingdom of my father," Jesus said. As they were talking she could heard a voice come from the throne, "This is my beloved Son, hear him," the voice said. Gabbi knew it was God talking. As he talked she bowed. A sense of worship came over her. She could not contain it, and she did not want to. She worshiped God and Jesus. As she was worshiping Jesus put his hand on her head as if to give her strength. With tears in her eyes, she began to say, "You are holy. You are holy Lord. Worthy. You are worthy Lord. Worthy to open the seals. Worthy to open the seals. You are worthy Lord, so open the seals." She knew that song did not come from her. "That was father singing through you Gabbi. Judgment time is coming," Jesus said. "What do you mean?" Gabbi asked. "Father gave me permission to open the seals of the book," Jesus said. "Book. What book?" Gabbi asked. "Your book. The book Gabriel told you he could not show you," Jesus said. Suddenly a book appeared on the bench in front of them sealed. Jesus took the seal off the book and opened it. He began to show Gabbi what God wrote about her.

At the top of the page were the words The Price. "Look here," Jesus said as he pointed. As she looked she noticed the name Deborah after her name. She looked up at Jesus and shrugged her shoulders. She did not know what this meant. "In the book of Judges, there was a girl named Deborah. She was the only woman judge in Israel. She sat under a tree as she judged Israel.

God brought victory to Israel through her. You are the Deborah of your generation. You will experience great victories. Not only will I back you up, but all of Heaven and the Court of Heaven will back you. No other person will be favored in these courts as you are Gabbi," Jesus explained to her.

He let her know this favor will not come cheap. This favor will come with a price attached to it. She will lose friends over this favor. Suddenly a voice came from the throne," I have given you favor my daughter. Favor treading in my courts. Favor to prophecy to dead things and watch them come to life. Favor speaking to mountains and watching them move. This favor comes at a hefty price. I am with you and in you. Walk in me and I will walk with you; saith the Lord thy God." "For I will turn circumstances around for you and your family. I will turn your mourning into joy. Trust in me with all your heart and see what I will do for you. This is your season and your time. Shine bright for me and watch me; saith the Lord thy God."

After God spoke to her Kathryn Kuhlman appeared in the Courts. Gabbi knew who she was because her dad read some of her books, and she remembered seeing her picture on the book covers. Why was she here? It did not take long before Gabbi knew the answer. " The price is great to walk in the mantles God placed on you," Kathryn said. "What do you mean?" Gabbi asked. "There will be many experiences of being lonely. You will be misunderstood. You will lose friends. So many things you will have to give up to walk this precious way," Kathryn told her. "Always remember Gabbi, God will not take you to it if he was not going to help you through it," Kathryn went on to say.

This made sense to Gabbi. She knew she took a lot of ridicule when she stood up for Olivia. All the names people called her hurt, but at the same time she knew she did the right thing. This knowledge made the hurts go away. If she had to lose friends to help her brother so be it. Friends come and go. They are replaceable, but family is permanent. You have many friends, but only one family.

"Gabbi, I paid a huge price to walk in the anointing. My husband left me. I ran out of churches. I was a very lonely woman in life. What made it all worth it? The anointing. Watching people get healed was worth it. I formed a close relationship with the Holy Ghost. You must form that same close relationship. He will help me when no one else can. When you are lonely, the Holy Ghost will be your comforter. The price is heavy, but with the help of the Holy Ghost, you can endure. The word tells you, "He that endures to the end shall be saved." There is salvation in enduring. So, be honored to take part in suffering for God. He will make your suffering seem lighter. Trust the process Gabbi, and let him lead you in every area of your life," Kathryn said as she suddenly vanished.

The moment Kathryn left a girl appeared in the Courts. She had a family resemblance. She looked a lot like her dad. She had thick black hair that went all the way down her spine. She was as tall as dad was. "Hi, my name is Holly. I am your sister," Holly said. "Dad never mentioned I had another sister," Gabbi said.

Holly was not surprised. No one mentioned her after she died because she was undeveloped her death. Her mother had a miscarriage when Holly was only three weeks. "My mom was pregnant with me after JR died. I was in her belly for three weeks, Jesus told me, then I died. I was a sign to dad and mom that they were not meant for each other. I know it sounds weird Gabbi, but dad was supposed to save himself for your mom, but with the age gap this was impossible at the time. My mom losing me was the final straw in her feelings for dad. She had a fake love for dad because in her mind love had children, and she lost two. JR and I watch over her because she is our mother, but we play an intricate role in dad's life. Do you know why Gabbi? It is because of the mantle dad carries. I'm here to tell you the same mantle is on you, but it is greater than his mantle," Holly said.

Gabbi was amazed at the beauty of Holly. She never knew she had another sister, but seeing her for the first time was worth all the mystery that now surrounds her. "What is JR like?" Gabbi asked. "Oh Gabbi, he is so funny. You've met uncle Kenny, right?" Holly asked. "Yes," Gabbi snickered. "Imagine JR like uncle Kenny. He is so funny and full of life. He makes Jesus laugh all the time. As funny as he is, there is also a side to him that is like dad. He can be very stoic when need be. That is the mantle he carries," Holly said. As Holly left she hugged Gabbi. "Go with God little sis," Holly said as she disappeared.

Gabbi and Jesus stood alone in the Courts. He continued telling her about the price she had to pay. He let her know she was not going to have very many friends on earth. Many of her friends will leave her as soon as the next day. It was not that they didn't like her, they just did not understand what she was walking in. The school knew Gabbi was different. She stood out, but in a good way. Many of her peers wanted what she had, but they did not know how to go about asking how to get it. This was going to cause them to leave her. Some of those that leave her will also persecute her in a big way.

Her brother was going to misbehave in greater ways. Satan was going to use him in any way he could try and discourage Gabbi. She had to keep her faith and trust in God higher than she ever had. That faith and trust were going to propel her into greatness. She knew she was ready for the challenge but was a little hesitant because of the factor of the unknown. What if she cracked under pressure? What if she failed her assignment?

The next day started out like any normal day. Her friends at school were hanging out with her having fun. That afternoon after lunch Olivia began questioning Gabbi's loyalty as a friend. She did not understand why Gabbi was drawn to Melissa and thought Gabbi abandoned her. The more Gabbi tried explaining to Olivia she was still her friend, the more Olivia wanted to argue. Finally after an hour of bickering Olivia said, "I don't think we can be friends anymore Gabbi. You're a sweet girl, but this God thing is getting a little much. I don't know him like that, and really don't know if I want to." This news hurt Gabbi to the core. She prayed with Olivia. Led her to the Lord, or so she thought. After all Olivia experienced and saw, how can she just turn her back like that? What about being friends till the end? Gabbi guessed this was the end.

After school Gabbi saw something that broke her heart. She saw Olivia smoking. Olivia had taken up a friendship with some bad girls from the Junior High. Gabbi watched as Olivia lit the cigarette and started smoking. She was hanging all over one of the boys in the group. Gabbi was sick watching Olivia and this boy. Why would Olivia sell her experience she had in God for a little fun in the world. She was only eight- years- old. She was too young for this. What was Gabbi going to do? She decided the only thing she could do was pray.

The next day at school Gabbi's class had a Math test. Olivia was caught cheating in the test. Her teacher escorted Olivia to the Principal's office. Once in the office, Olivia put all the blame on Gabbi. Olivia claimed Gabbi made the cheat sheet and gave it to Olivia so she could pass the test. The teacher found that answer hard to believe, so she called Gabbi into the office. Gabbi explained she never made a cheat sheet, and she did not give anything to Olivia before the test. The Principal and the teacher believed Gabbi, and Olivia was sent home from school for out of school detention. This made their relationship worse, as Olivia told Gabbi she would retaliate for getting in trouble. As Gabbi walked back to the class Jesus said, "Fear not Gabbi. She will not retaliate one bit. Be patient, for I will save her to the uttermost and you will get your friend back, but she will be sold out to me." "Amen," Gabbi said.

That night she was interceding in prayer for Olivia. She travailed so hard sweat was pouring off her. "Oh God, save Olivia," Gabbi cried. As she prayed two angels came and sit on her bed beside her. They were ministering strength to her as she prayed for Olivia. Suddenly, Jesus appeared in front of her. "Daughter," Jesus said. Gabbi looked up and saw Jesus standing in front of her. "I want to give you a big test to see where your heart is," Jesus said. Gabbi stopped praying to give Jesus her undivided attention. "If I was to ask you to give Melissa your brand new bicycle would you do it?" Jesus asked her. Before she could answer Jesus went on, "If I asked you to give her all of your allowance each week but $1 would you do it?" Without hesitation Gabbi answered, "For you Jesus I would do anything." Jesus smiled at her answer and nodded because he knew the answer she would give.

"I am going to heal your brother. The degree of obedience from you will determine whether I give him a miracle or just a healing. Let me explain. Should I ask you to give up your bicycle and you did it immediately without complaining, he would get a miracle. If you murmured and complained, but went ahead and did it, he would get a healing. The healing would not be instant and could take years. Your obedience will either move me or slow me. That my daughter is your big test," Jesus said. After he told her that, Jesus and the angels disappeared, leaving Gabbi alone in her room. Wow she was fixing to be tested. Is this part of the price she was to pay to walk in what God wanted her to walk in? She did not know for sure, but one thing she knew she had to pass this test. Joseph's healing is on the line, and she can not let him down. Ever.

CHAPTER 3
SCHOOL HOUSE ROCK

The following week Olivia returned to school. Gabbi hoped Olivia would be different than she was the week before. Gabbi believed Olivia was going through a phase, and soon she would see the light. Olivia was meaner than she was before she got detention. She walked in the classroom and started picking on Melissa. "You took my best friend away from me. You and your family are poor and worthless. Timmy didn't deserve you," Olivia mouthed to Melissa. This made Melissa cry uncontrollably. "Why did you say that to me?" Melissa cried. "Because it is true," Olivia said.

Gabbi overheard the conversation and took up for Melissa. "Olivia, how could you?" Gabbi asked. "When your father was killed I took up for you against Roger. Now, you are going to be mean to Melissa because I befriended her. She lost her little brother and you do this to her? You were at her house comforting her when Timmy died. She doesn't deserve this. You will answer to God," Gabbi said.

"How do you know God exists?" Olivia asked. "Olivia, after all you saw in dreams and visions. How can you stand there and ask me that question. Are you serious?" Gabbi asked. "It was a phase Gabbi. Just a phase," Olivia said. "Really?" Gabbi asked. Olivia refused to talk to Gabbi anymore that day. Her and her friends walked around the whole day whispering about Gabbi and Melissa. This did not deter Gabbi. She knew she was paying the price for the walk she was experiencing. Joseph was going to be healed if she does what God tells her. This drove Gabbi harder than ever before.

That night Gabbi was sleeping. She awoke in the Court of Heaven. The courtroom was packed. On the left side were all the host of Hell. The smell coming from that side of the room could turn your stomach. The smell of death was so strong on their side of the room. They sat and talked among themselves. She could not understand what they were saying. All she could hear was hyena noises coming from them.

On the right side sat the Cloud of Witnesses. They were joined by the disciples and apostles. The angelic host was standing along the wall from the floor all the way to the top of the room. At the prosecution table Lucifer was sitting with two other demons. At the defense table Gabbi was seated with Jesus and the Holy Ghost. Sitting in the jury box was Olivia. She was chained from head to toe. Next to her were two demon guards.

Court was called to session. The judge looked at Lucifer and said, "What is so important Lucifer that you called this special session?" "I want Olivia's soul," Lucifer said. "Objection!" Yelled the Holy Spirit. "Sustained," the judge said. "Oh, let me explain," Lucifer said. "Go ahead," the judge said. Lucifer gets out of his chair and walks in front of Olivia. "She gave me the right to ask for her soul. The conversations she has been having with Gabbi gives me access to her soul. She claims there is nothing to this God. She doesn't believe in you anymore. Also, she is smoking and having sex with an older boy. She's a sinner. A sinner, I say," Lucifer said.

Suddenly Gabbi stands up and points to Jesus. "Yes, she said those things. Yes, she did those things, but all have sinned and come short of the Glory of God. Even you, Lucifer sinned against God. The difference between you and her is the blood of Jesus," Gabbi protested. "Stop. Stop now," Lucifer demanded. "As I was saying, "Gabbi said. "The blood of Jesus cleanses Olivia from her sins. No matter how bad Olivia has been, I plead the blood of Jesus over her life," Gabbi said.

As she spoke blood an angel walked over to Olivia and took blood from what looked like a chalice, and with a hyssop applied the blood all over Olivia. From the top of her head to the soles of her feet, the blood was heavily applied. "Not guilty," the judge said. "Your request Lucifer is denied. She is my child. She may have made mistakes and said some awful things, but her heart belongs to me. Loose her and let her go," the judge demanded. As he said that the chains fell off of Olivia and she disappeared. Suddenly Gabbi was teleport-ed from the courtroom to a bone yard.

In the bone yard she saw Olivia lying on the ground. Her body was decayed, and all that was left was a bunch of dry bones. "Prophesy to the bones Gabbi," the Holy Spirit said. "Oh bones of Olivia, I command you to hear the word of the Lord. You are not a sinner, but you belong to God. He has released you from the clutches of Satan. I prophesy to your bones that they come together now in the name of Jesus," Gabbi said. As she spoke the bones came back together. Flesh appeared on the bones in the appearance of Olivia. She lay there on the ground with no life in her.

"Prophesy to the four winds and command life to come into Olivia," Holy Spirit said. "I command the winds of the North, South, East and West to blow life into Olivia now, in the name of Jesus. Suddenly, the wind began to blow from all four directions.

As the wind blew life came back into Olivia and she stood up. In this vision she began walking, and leaping and praising God. She was not bound anymore, but she was free. Instantly Gabbi was back in her bed sound asleep. She operated in both mantles and Olivia, whether she knew it or not, was set free.

The next day Gabbi noticed a difference in Olivia. She was nice to Gabbi. She was nice to Melissa too. Gabbi knew something took place, but she wanted to hear it fro Olivia. "Gabbi, Can I talk to you?" Olivia asked. "Of course," Gabbi said. "I want to apologize to you and Melissa for the way I have been acting. It wasn't me at all. I was hurt because you seemed to pay more attention to Melissa. My sister's friends did not help either. They got me smoking and liking one of her friends. Last night I dreamed I was in a car crash. I dreamed the boy I liked stole a car and we went for a joy ride. He ended up crashing, and I dreamed I died. While in that dream Jesus appeared to me. He did not get on to me for the things I did, he told me he loved me and wanted me back. I woke up from that dream and repented. Now I'm repenting to you and Melissa," Olivia said.

"Olivia, I did pay attention to Melissa, but you're still my friend. I can have you and Melissa as friends. Last night I was in the Court of Heaven fighting for your soul. Satan had you bound in chains, and wanted to take your soul. God denied his request. Then I was taken to the graveyard where your bones were. I prophesied life back into you. I'm not surprised you had that dream. I forgive you," Gabbi said.

While they were talking Gabbi's brother Joseph walked up. Joseph is four years older than Gabbi. He thinks on a different level than his age, but has a heart of gold. He struggles more than any kid in school. He has his good days and bad days, but overall, he is a good kid.

Joseph is a tall handsome boy with think black curly hair. Every time a person sees him he has a smile on his face. Sometimes he can be annoying to Gabbi, but she tries to overlook it. Joseph likes Melissa. He knows she is younger than him, but that doesn't deter him. Melissa likes Joseph as well. In fact, when Joseph acts up at school Melissa is the one to put him back on the straight and narrow. One day last week Joseph was mad at a boy in his class. He started cussing and throwing things in the hallway. Melissa heard all the commotion and went to investigate. There Joseph was with a chair in his hand getting ready to throw it down the hall. Melissa ran up beside him and began talking him down. Sudden;y, Joseph began using his coping skills and put the chair down. Joseph had to go to the principal's office and was sent home for two days. He is grateful Melissa showed up when she did because he was going to hurt someone.

No one understands Joseph the way Melissa does. Timmy used to have the same struggles. He used to throw fits in stores if he didn't get what he wanted. His mom tried everything to help Timmy, but nothing seemed to help. Timmy was kicked out of three schools for his behaviour. On one occasion he hit the teacher in the head with one of his matchbox cars he brought to school. A day before coming to the school the kids currently attend, Timmy had a meltdown in Dollar General because he wanted candy but his mother told him no. Their mother tried to go easy on him because of his bouts with leukemia. She figured he was acting out because he was sick. His life changed the day he met Jesus, and the day before his homecoming.

The night he met Jesus he had a fabulous night. He shared his toys with Tommy, which is something he struggled with. He wanted to go for ice cream since someone donated money to them. His mom allowed it, but laid the law down to him. Timmy bought what his mom told him to with no incident. He acted as if he knew the next day he was going to die. Melissa shared that story with Gabbi, Joseph and Olivia. Gabbi cried as Melissa told the story. She missed Timmy so much it hurt. In a way, Gabbi liked Timmy. She liked Tommy more, but she was kind of sweet on Timmy. Now Timmy watches over all of the kids.

As they were talking Jesus asked Gabbi to do something she knew he probably would do. "Gabbi, I know you love me, and will do whatever I ask. I want you to buy Melissa, Joseph and Olivia's lunch today. Olivia's mom lost her job and they do not have the money for her to eat today. She will not say anything because she is afraid you will judge her for it," Jesus said. Without hesitation, Gabbi took all three kids to the lunchroom and spent all of her allowance on them. She had to obey what Jesus said.

While in Math class Jesus spoke to Gabbi again, "I want you to give Melissa your bicycle. You are going to get a better one." Gabbi nodded her head in agreement with what Jesus said. After school Gabbi took Melissa to her house and gave her the bicycle. Melissa cried tears of joy because no one ever got her a bicycle before. This was the first one she ever had. Gabbi felt real good knowing she helped Melissa out. After Melissa left, a car pulled up in Gabbi's driveway. A woman got out of her car and opened the trunk. Inside the trunk was the bicycle Gabbi always wanted. She had a red twenty inch Schwinn Frozen bicycle. This bicycle had all the bells and whistles. It had a horn, a light on it, reflectors fro the front to the back, including the wheels. Gabbi learned the value in listening to that small voice inside her heart. In addition to her bicycle, Joseph received one. The lady reached in her purse and gave Gabbi an envelope to give to her parents. Her mom opened the envelope, and inside was a note. The note said, " I will bring the deed to the house by later on today." Inside the note was a check for five thousand dollars. Her mom cried joyfully. They were needing a new place to live because where they were was unfit.

An hour passed and the lady came back. In her hand was the deed to a two story five bedroom house located a block away from the school. "I was cooking supper and suddenly a voice told me to give your kids brand new bicycles. As I went and bought the bicycles, the voice told me to write you the check. As I was writing the check, the voice told me to give you the deed to this house. This house belonged to my husband's mother. She died three months ago, and he died a month ago. I had no interest living in that house as I am happy where I am. I was looking for a buyer when your name came in my head. Enjoy the house," the lady said. Gabbi's mom hugged the lady and thanked her. "You have no idea what this means to my family," Gabbi's mom said.

As Gabbi was praying that night she thanked God for allowing her to be obedient. She helped Melissa with a bicycle, and in return her and Joseph not only got a new bicycle, but money, and a new house. "Obedience is better than sacrifice," Jesus said. " I want you to give Olivia your brand new life size Elsa doll tomorrow," Jesus said. "Okay, I will," Gabbi said as she went to sleep.

The next day was Saturday. All of the kids gather at Gabbi's house on Saturday to play. When Olivia came over Gabbi took her aside. "I want to give you my Elsa doll," Gabbi said. "Olivia couldn't believe it. She always wanted one of those dolls. Her mom bought her one last year for Christmas, but the other night it was stolen. Someone broke into their house and took all of Olivia's dolls, and Elsa was one of the dolls take. They have an idea who done it, but cannot prove it. Olivia was going to have to wait until Christmas this year to get another one. God works in mysterious ways.

On Monday Joseph had another episode. He was on the playground playing with Melissa when a boy came up and started calling him names. Instead of ignoring him, Joseph swung at him. A fight erupted between the two boys. Joseph grabbed the boy by his left ear and hurt him. Melissa stepped in and calmed Joseph down. Both boys ended up getting suspended for five days.

That night Gabbi was interceding for Joseph. Suddenly, she and Joseph were both escorted into Heaven. They were standing in a room with a huge throne. Sitting on the throne was a huge man. He was very ancient looking. His hair was white as sheep's wool. His hair went past his shoulders. His eyes were a beautiful blue. When he looked at you, it appeared he could look into your soul. His eyes were the window of his soul, as his gaze was filled with love. His gaze could melt your heart. No matter what you were going through, one gaze from this man made everything good.

He was so radiant looking. There was lightning around the throne. As he moved the lightning flashed. Gabbi had never seen lightning up close. This lightning was a royal blue and when you looked at it it was very bright. "That's the glory of the Lord," an angel said. Around the throne angels were gathered around singing, "Holy, holy, holy, Lord God almighty. Who was, and is, and is, to come." The man enjoyed the praises. It was as if he was living inside those praises.

"I am Jehovah," the man said. "I am Jesus' father, and I want to be yours too," Jehovah said. "Why am I here?" Joseph asked. " I brought you here Joseph to tell you how much I love you," Jehovah said. "You do?" Joseph asked. "Yes son, I love you very much. I know what you are struggling with in life, but my love for you is just as strong as ever,"Jehovah said. "I've been very bad," Joseph said. "Joseph, no matter how bad you have been, my love for you never changes. Ask your sister Gabbi," Jehovah said.

"I told you Joseph," Gabbi said. "Gabbi, I am proud of you," Jehovah said. "The way you bought your friends and brother's lunches. The way you gave up your bicycle to Melissa. That daughter is love. My son knows a lot about love. My word says "Greater love hath no man have than a man lay down his life for his friends," Jehovah said. Gabbi was amazed at how awesome Jehovah looked. This is the first time she ever laid eyes on him. Even in the Court of Heave his face was not seen. All she could see was a figure. Now she was looking at him face to face, and she has not dropped dead. "Jesus made you a promise Gabbi, and I brought you and Joseph her to fulfill that promise," Jehovah said.

Suddenly they were in a room with a pottery station. Suddenly Jesus appeared in the room and sat down at the wheel. He motioned for Joseph to come over and stand beside him. Joseph looked like he was scared as he approached Jesus. "Fear not Joseph," Jesus said. Suddenly Joseph had peace. As he stood beside Jesus, he noticed Jesus working on the wheel. He took a piece of clay and began to mold it. The piece he was working on had a crack in it. Jesus took the clay off the wheel, wadded it up and start all over. Jesus worked the clay until it became a beautiful piece of pottery. He took the pot off the wheel and put it in the oven. After a while Jesus took the pot out of the oven, and it was all nice and shiny, a beautiful piece fit for use. "This is what I am going to do for you Joseph. You may be flawed right now, but when I am done with you, a vessel you will be that I can use for my glory. I am going to transform your mind, and you will have my mind in you, I am going to take your heart that seems to make bad choices, and give you my heart, and you will learn to act like I would," Jesus said. Joseph was awestruck at what he was witnessing. He never knew such love as he is feeling right now. How could he? He had never been in the presence of love like he was now. "I am love Joseph," Jesus said. "Gabbi as you have obeyed my voice, I am healing your brother now," Jesus said. Suddenly, Jesus tenderly and lovingly put his hand on the side of Joseph's head. " Come forth," Jesus commanded. It was like a switch turned on in Joseph. He began looking different. He had a glow to him. He was very calm after Jesus touched him. Gabbi knew Jesus did something wonderful for Joseph. She could not put her finger on it, but she knew it was true. Suddenly she woke up in her bed.

Joseph seemed to be better the next day. He ignored the kids that called him names. One boy pushed him and tried to start a fight with him. Joseph looked at him, smiled, and said "I forgive you." The boy was stunned at Joseph's reaction. He asked Joseph why he did that. Joseph responded,"Jesus forgave me for all the bad I have done. I forgive you for pushing me and trying to get me to fight you. I'm not going to fight you or anyone else, I am going to love and pray for you." The boy stood there with tears streaming down his face. "I don't know what happened to you Joseph, but whatever it is I need and want it," the boy said. Joseph called Gabbi over to where he was. He told her what happened, and Gabbi led the boy to the Lord.

It is amazing what one touch from Jesus can do. A touch can take someone that likes to get into trouble and transform them into a peace loving person. Such is the case with Joseph. For the rest of the year Joseph did not get into anymore fights. His new attitude transformed his classroom in ways no one ever thought possible. The teacher and principal was amazed at his transformation. At times they scratched their heads wondering where Joseph went. He did not go anywhere in the flesh. His ind and attitude was transformed by God. He went from D's and F's in school to A's and B's. Reading and Math used to be his worst subjects. Ever since his encounter with Jesus, he excelled in those subjects tremendously.

No one ever expected Joseph to be anything other than a trouble maker. Joseph, with the help of Jesus, proved everyone wrong. Melissa became his girlfriend and the only one that could talk sense into him when he needed it. Even though she was younger than him by four years, her intelligence and spunk filled in the age gap. Gabbi never dreamed when she gave up her bicycle and bought the four kids their lunch just how much of an impact obedience would have on Joseph's life. She is forever grateful she listened to the voice of the Lord. For her the story did not end. For Gabbi, there is more. The best is yet to come. Soon she will change not only her school and brother, but other schools and other families will experience transformation by the obedience of Gabbi. But now she must go through her time of testing to be more like Jesus. With the help of Jesus she can endure until the end.

CHAPTER 4
TIME OF TESTING AND MIRACLES

A week after Joseph was touched by God, an angel appeared to Gabbi in the middle of the night. Before this appearance by the angel, Gabbi witnessed to four of her friends while they were playing at her house. Three of them received the Lord for the first time, and the other one made a fresh commitment. They were watching the movie The Passion of the Christ. As the movie was playing the Holy Spirit moved strong in the living room. Gabbi noticed two of the girls were crying uncontrollably. She asked them if they knew the Lord, which they responded they did not. She asked them if they wanted to pray, and they did, accepting Jesus into their hearts. The other girl told Gabbi how she once went to church. She was baptized in water and filled with the Holy Ghost. Setbacks happened in her life, and she backslid on God. She prayed with Gabbi and made a fresh commitment. It seemed revival was breaking out in Gabbi's school.

When the angel appeared, he told Gabbi "It is time for you to be tested. God wants to know what is in your heart. He wants to know if you are true or not, although he already knows. This testing is not for his sake, but for your sake." Jesus appeared beside the angel and told her, "Gabbi I'm going to shake things up. Some of your friends are going to leave you, because they are not really for you. As they leave I am going to send more. These friends are not going to be from the top echelon but they will be the lowest of the low. That is who I am drawn to. You will be in the Gethsemane moment of your life. I want to see if you a\re willing to have my father's will in your life above your own. You will pass the test." The angel and Jesus suddenly departed.

The next day at school, it seemed like a hurricane hit her life. Some of her best friends suddenly turned against her. The teacher told the class Olivia ran away from home last night and Family Services took her to another town and she would not be coming back the rest of the year. This devastated Gabbi. Olivia was doing so good. What would have caused her to do this? No more talks. No more praying around the flag pole before class, because Olivia as gone. She still had Melissa to pray with, but Olivia made it entertaining. Some of the prayers she prayed made Gabbi smile and shake her head. Did she really have Melissa as a friend, or was she going to leave her too? Melissa and Joseph were now boyfriend and girlfriend, and how was that going to affect her friendship with Gabbi?

Gabbi had a Math test that day. Normally Gabbi does good on her tests. This particular test was a pitfall for her. Everything was going great during the test. Suddenly, she hit a snag. There was five problems she did not remember how to do. Fractions were always stumping for her. Of all things to put multiple questions on, fractions were those items. This caused Gabbi to bomb her test. She didn't only bomb her test, she bombed it miserably. Instead of getting all bent out of shape, she thanked the Lord because at least she tried. She thanked the Lord for the friends she lost as well. She knew there would be friends come into her life that really needed Jesus. She had a lot to thank God for. Melissa was her new best friend. Joseph was really doing great. No more fights. He quit having outbursts. If bombing a test and losing friends were for Melissa and Joseph's benefit, it was worth it.

Later on that day she noticed a girl in the hallway. This girl had matted blonde hair that looked like had never been washed. Her clothes were tattered and had holes in them. The pants she had on were short. The legs went up an inch from her shoes revealing dingy socks. "This is who I want to touch," Jesus told Gabbi. While everyone looked at her and laughed, Gabbi walked up and befriended her. Gabbi found out her name was Melinda. Gabbi marched her to the lunchroom and bought Melinda something to eat and drink. After school, Gabbi called her mother and invited Melinda over for a hot supper.

Within an hour after Melinda went to Gabbi's house, Melinda's mother picked her up. Melinda's mother shared their story. Melinda's father used to have a great job. He was a pilot for a major airline. A year ago they found out he had cancer. He fought hard for over a year. Two weeks ago he died. Melinda's mother is employed at a fast food restaurant. She wanted a better job, but she does not have a high school diploma, so no one will hire her. She became pregnant with Melinda her freshman year of high school, and had to drop out. Her family was too poor to be able to afford her GED, so she was never able to get her diploma. Gabbi's mom called around getting prices for GED classes. As soon as she found a place she could comfortably pay for, she enrolled Melinda's mom into the classes and paid for them. Gabbi could feel Jesus smiling at her. She passed her test.

That night as Gabbi was minding her own business in her bedroom that all familiar voice came calling. "Give Melinda your bicycle and you go without one until I tell you different," the voice said. Gabbi got told her mom and dad what she was supposed to do, and immediately took her bicycle and gave it to Melinda. To some of her classmates, this was strange. It was strange to Gabbi too, but obedience was better than sacrifice. When she returned home from giving her bicycle to Melinda, in her driveway sat a brand new bicycle.

As Gabbi was admiring her bicycle God told her to go find her dad and stand by him. "I have a word for your dad. I want to heal his inner man," God said. She rushed at once and found him. As she stood beside him the spirit of the Lord entered her mouth. "Every wall in your life is coming down. Brick by brick, stronghold by stronghold, they are coming down. I see the hurts, the deep hurts that have crippled your ministry all your life. I see the rejection you have experienced from childhood to adulthood. My spirit is going to be in you like a hurricane and everything that holds you down will be destroyed. Your ministry is not over. Your ministry is not a failure. The hurts that have held you captive is causing delay in the things I want to do for you. I say no more delay, because, I am destroying the spirit of delay in your life. Forgive yourself my son. Forgive yourself for all the times you rebelled against my word. Forgive yourself for feeling like you were an outcast. Forgive yourself and live, because the moment you repented I forgave all of that and cast it far from me. Why haven't you? Dwell in my courts like I ordained you to. Stop allowing Satan to tell you your self worth. You know your self worth for yourself and he will not have the power to name your worth. Forgive your real mother son. It is crippling your anointing. As you forgive yourself and others, I will begin to break the chains that have you held back and bound. Love your family like you have never before. For behold I am giving you a new found love even now. I say unto you this is the first day of your new life in me. Walk in that new life and see what I will do for you, saith the Lord".

The presence of the Lord filled the entire house as Gabbi was being used to speak into her dad's life. There was a reverential awe in the house. All dad could do was kneel in the presence and repent. With tears in his eyes and hands lifted high in the air, he repented for all the things God spoke to him about. Suddenly, the spirit of the Lord entered him and he began to preach the message he had been hiding inside him since he was seventeen years old. As he began to preach Joseph, Gabbi, and their mom gathered around to listen. Suddenly, Joseph began to speak in another language. The heavy cloud of glory rested on the house for several hours. The family soaked in this glory cloud, and miracles began to happen.

"Speak to your mom," God said to Gabbi. "My daughter I have called you. It is not a figment of your imagination, I the Lord called you. I see the hurts. I see the wounds and the scars that go deep. I see the times you lay on your pillow and cry yourself to sleep. I say unto you "daughter arise" I am breaking depression off of your life. You will have joy unspeakable and full of glory. I am giving you beauty for ashes. The oil of joy for mourning. The garment of praise for the spirit of heaviness. You are not worthless, you are full of worth. Walk in that worth, and as you walk in that worth, my glory shall overshadow you. You are going to do the Kathryn Kuhlman of your generation. Believe me and walk in me, saith the Lord."

Gabbi turned to Joseph and said, "The spirit of David rests upon you. You will slay your Goliath once and for all." As she finished ministering she fell in the floor. When she hit the floor she was immediately taken to a banquet room. In this room there was a huge table. The table went from one end of the room to the other. On the table were all kinds of fruits, nuts, and meat. She loves grapes, and the grapes that were on the table were huge. These grapes were bigger than what she could get at the grocery store. There were purple grapes, red grapes, white grapes, and other various colors of grapes. Colors she never knew existed. The table was not thrown together. The table was carefully organized. The fruit was arranged not only by type, but also by size. The fruit was arranged with her favorite fruit being first. They went from big to small. The fruit she did not care for was small. She loves all kinds of nuts, and there were nuts she never knew existed. The table cloth was royal purple. Gabbi loves purple, but the purple she sees everyday does not compare to royal purple. She was awestruck by what she was seeing.

Standing at the end of this massive table was Jesus. He had on a white silk robe, a purple sash and a crown on his head. Girded around his waist was a towel. "Come and dine," Jesus said. As Gabbi approached the table Jesus began offering her food. "Partake of this purple grape. This is the fruit of love," Jesus said. He offered her various fruits naming them as he went along. "I gave you a taste of all the nine fruits of the spirit that are on this table. Each type of fruit represents a type of the spirit," Jesus said. As she finished eating he pulled out a chair in the middle of the room. "Sit her daughter," Jesus said. As Gabbi sat down Jesus knelt in front of her. There suddenly appeared a basin of water. Jesus took the towel from around his waste and put it on his lap. He lifted Gabbi's feet and put them in the water. The water felt good on Gabbi's feet. She has felt velvet before, but this water felt like a light velvet. It was so soft and warm on her feet. "I am bathing you in the water of life," Jesus said. He began washing her feet. As he washed, she began to feel all the weight she had been carrying around life off of her. The weights from the testing she had been going through was lifting off of her. He went from her feet to her head. He produced a vial of oil. He gently poured the oil on her head "I have anointed you for service," Jesus said. The oil went on her head, down her face, all the way to her feet that were still in the water. "The oil represents the spirit. You are drenched in the spirit of my father," Jesus said. For the first time in a long time Gabbi felt clean and refreshed. "You are getting ready to do exploits for the kingdom. Miracles, signs and wonders will follow you," Jesus said. As he told her that he breathed upon her. "Receive the Holy Ghost," Jesus said. Suddenly Gabbi woke herself up speaking in tongues. She does not know how long she was speaking in tongues, because when she is transported into these visions time stands still.

The family was gathered around Gabbi watching her commune in the Holy Ghost. Over Joseph's head Gabbi saw a beautiful white dove. Joseph the same glow on him JR had on him. "Is he going to die to?" Gabbi asked herself. "Not physically, as he has many years left. He died and has experienced a new spiritual birth. That is the reason for the glow," Jesus said. Gabbi was relieved to hear Joseph was going to be around a long time. "How long have I been on the floor?" Gabbi asked. "Four hours," her mom said. "Dad preached an awesome message, and when he got done I preached too. That is when you began to speak in tongues," her mom told her. "Wow! Praise God," Gabbi said.

CHAPTER 5
IN HIS SERVICE

Gabbi formed a Friends in Christ club in her neighborhood. She invited Melissa, Tommy and Joseph to attend the meetings. These meetings were not typical meetings that normal clubs have. They were deciding how they were going to feed the kids at school that didn't have the money to buy lunch. It was very important to Gabbi that no kid go hungry at school. She took the vision of the banquet table very serious. She knew it was her job to make sure God's creation was taken care of. Feeding them was the least she could do to help take care of God's creation.

In one of the meetings Melissa invited her cousin to attend. Her cousin's name was Mateo. Mateo was of Mexican descent. His aunt was married to an Hispanic man. Mateo was not well liked in his community. He was what people considered the scum of the earth. There was rumors going around that Mateo was a Wiccan. He dressed in all black. He had an earring in his ear, and painted his fingernails black. Mateo was older than Gabbi and Melissa. He was around Joseph's age. He seemed like a nice young man, but was weird. This did not deter Gabbi at all. She saw something in him that no one else saw, he had a soul that God needed to touch. She made it her mission to try and touch him. It would be easy to be like the in- crowd and shun him. She has a sign hanging on her wall that she thinks of when she runs across people that others shun. The sign reads WWJD. What

Would Jesus Do? When he showed up at the meeting, Joseph could not believe his eyes. Joseph had just been filled with the Holy Ghost, so he was still capable of making mistakes. "Why did Melissa bring him?" Joseph asked. "Joseph, stop. WWJD?" Gabbi replied. This made Joseph stop and he tried to understand the situation.

As the meeting progressed Gabbi wanted to have prayer. Mateo became uncomfortable about praying. "Jesus loves you Mateo," Gabbi said. "No one loves me," Mateo said. "Why do you say that?" Gabbi asked. "I'm so misunderstood and misjudged," Mateo said. "What do you mean?" Gabbi asked. "I'm not Wiccan, I just love wearing black," Mateo said. "I was abused as a child. I feel like I'm the invisible man. No one likes me or wants to be around me. I don't get to play sports because I am different. This is the first place I have ever been invited to. So, I wear black as a way to express how I am feeling," Mateo said with tears streaming down his face. She could see the pain in his eyes. He was hurting and no one understood him. How could people be so cruel?

"Mateo, Jesus is one man that loves you. He loves you so much he died for you," Gabbi said. "I would never die for someone like me," Mateo said. "Jesus is not like we are. He loves us even when we don't love ourselves," Gabbi said. "I hate myself," Mateo cried. "There is so much good in you Mateo, but you have allowed what people said about you or done to you cloud your vision. Jesus loves you so much. He hurts when you hurt," Gabbi replied. "No one has ever done that for me," Mateo said. "Well mister, Jesus does. He wants nothing more than to wrap his arms around you and love on you," Gabbi said. "Mateo, she is telling you the truth," Melissa said.

"Remember when Timmy told your mom he accepted Jesus the night before he died?" Melissa asked. "Yes, I remember, and I thought he was nuts. I miss Tim man," Mateo cried. "Timmy did not think anyone could love him because of what happened to him. When he met Jesus it changed him. He never had a song to sing. The day of his death, he sang songs of healing to mom and all of us in the room. Mateo, mom even accepted Jesus because of Timmy," Melissa told him. Mateo sat quiet for a moment taking in everything he was being told.

"I have never told anyone how much Timmy meant to me. I was mean to him at times, but I loved him as if he was the brother I never had. I would have died for Timmy. When I was told he had leukemia I was crushed. They told me it was in remission and I celebrated, until the day I was told it came back. Why him? Why Timmy? If God loved him, why did he allow him to suffer?" Mateo replied. "Jesus took him home so he would not suffer anymore. You said you would die for Timmy? Well, Jesus not only would, but he did die for you," Gabbi said. She shared with him the night Jesus allowed her to see what happened the day he died on the cross. She shared with him every detail she saw about the events. As she was explaining what she saw, she noticed Mateo was in tears. "Are you ready? Are you ready to accept Jesus?" Gabbi asked. "Yes, Yes I am," Mateo said. That day at the club meeting Mateo, a misunderstood and misjudged boy who only wanted to be loved met love. He gave his life to Jesus, and was instantly filled with the Holy Ghost. People on the outside of the garage where the meeting was being held could hear a ruckus. Many of the neighbors came into Gabbi's yard to investigate the noise. When they peeked their head into the garage, they noticed Mateo on his knees with his hands in the air, tear soaked eyes speaking in other tongues. Gabbi, Joseph and Melissa were around him shouting and dancing. Some of the on-lookers raised their hands to the sky as the glory of God came rushing through them. One of the neighbors came in and knelt beside Mateo and began to experience what Mateo was experiencing. God was moving in that garage.

Gabbi asked her pastor if he could baptize her, Joseph, Melissa and Mateo in water. When her pastor agreed, they went to the lake the following Sunday afternoon to be baptized. On the bank the church congregation gathered to witness the event. As the pastor and the participants got into the water the crowd began to sing There is a River. Suddenly, the lake area was filled with the glory of God. As they were being baptized, each of the kids came up speaking in tongues with the glory of God resting on them. In attendance was Melissa's aunt. She was also Mateo's mom. She got into the water and came up to the pastor and asked him what she had to do to be saved. The pastor and the kids lead her to the Lord. After they led her to the Lord she was baptized. When she came up she became drunk in the Holy Ghost. The pastor and another gentleman had to help her back to the bank. At the bank, Mateo's mom was still speaking in tongues. The crowd began to erupt in praise and thanksgiving. A little ways from the baptizing was a couple fishing. They noticed all the commotion and decided to investigate. By the time they left the investigation, they were saved, baptized and filled with the Holy Ghost. Revival was breaking out on the bank of the lake thanks to Gabbi's obedience.

If the lake was turned upside down for the Lord, imagine what would happen if the town became turned upside down for the Lord. Gabbi was quickly learning how being obedient pays off. Although she was eight years old, God was using her as if she was an adult. "Will you preach my word?" Jesus asked Gabbi at the baptism. "Yes, I will preach your word," Gabbi promised him.

CHAPTER 6
GABBI'S TESTIMONY

After Gabbi, Joseph, Melissa and Mateo were baptized Gabbi began sharing her testimony. She shared how Jesus first appeared to her. How she was taken to Heaven and shown the Heavenly library. She told people about the two roads, the one leading to Heaven and how there is no struggle on this path. The other path leads to Hell, and she shared how she watched the boy on the road to Hell carrying a heavy load. She hit home how he fell beneath that load and was trying to get up. She shared what she saw in Hell. She told this testimony to anyone that would listen.

On one particular Saturday she was at the park. There was such a crowd at the park you could shake it with a stick. Kids from all different races, family backgrounds, and ethnic backgrounds were in attendance. Suddenly, Gabbi felt that familiar nudge in her spirit. She gathered as many people around her as she could and began to tell them her testimony. As she began to share, the atmosphere began to change. No longer did kids want to play. No longer did adults want to talk, cuss, and act like hoodlums, all eyes and ears were on Gabbi. As she was sharing she could see ministering angels going from person to person touching them. She noticed one angel touched this little girl that had leg braces on and was on crutches. She suffered from Muscular Dystrophy. She watched the angel touch the girl's legs. She watched strength come into the girl's legs. Suddenly, the girl threw down her crutches and begin walking without them. As she walked, to Gabbi's amazement, the braces fell off the girl. The sight of this caused the crowd to be amazed. No one around Gabbi saw the angel do this. This work was invisible to the naked eye. Gabbi saw this miracle in the spirit with a spiritual eye.

As the crowd was watching the girl walk around Gabbi asked if anyone wanted to be saved. Hands went up all around the gathering. Gabbi took a deep breath and said, "Repeat after me. Father I come to you a sinner. Against you, and you alone have I sinned. I am truly and deeply sorry for my sins. Was me and cleanse me from my sins, and set me free. I will live for you and serve you to the best of my ability as long as I live. Take my name out of the Book of Death and write it in the Book of Life. I accept Jesus as my Lord and Savior now. In Jesus' name I am saved."

After the crowd prayed there was rejoicing. There was one couple in attendance that was at the park discussing their pending divorce. They were approaching their court date, so they were there trying to be civil with one another as they discussed their two children. As they were praying, Gabbi noticed two angels, one on the man's side and one on the woman's side. The angels were ministering to the couple. There were also two angels standing on both sides of the children administering what looked like first aid to them. She saw chains around the man. Suddenly, as he was praying another angel came and stood in front of him. In his hand was a key to the padlock. He took that key and unlocked the padlock. As the padlock was opened the chains fell off the man. After the prayer, the man took his wife and children and stood in front of the crowd that was gathered. "My wife and I are getting divorced. These two kids at our sides are our children. I am or I should say was addicted to pornography. I put it in front of my family. Instead of loving my wife as I should I put my love into this habit. This addiction caused me to cheat on my wife and she caught me. As we prayed a moment ago, something happened to me. I cannot explain it. I all of the sudden started hating pornography. I looked at my wife, and I saw her in a way I have never saw her before. Honey, I can't undo what I've done. All

I can do is change me now. I ask you to forgive me and give us another chance," the man said with tears rushing down his face. The woman looked at her soon to be ex- husband with tears in her eyes and said," Yes, I forgive you. I never wanted this divorce. I just couldn't stand to be second fiddle. When you cheated on me I was crushed. As I was praying I felt a release. All the hurt, anger and resentment I had for you disappeared. When I looked at you I saw a new man. I didn't see what you did, but what you are going to do. Yes, I forgive you and I want to stay married now and forever," the woman said.

There were other reports. God went to the park and touched a bunch of people that had no hope. He healed the broken hearts and set the captive free. Gabbi learned another valuable lesson on being obedient to the Lord.

CHAPTER 7
THE JOURNEY

That night Gabbi was reflecting on what took place. Suddenly she was standing in Heaven. She was standing beside a beautiful flowing river. The water was a beautiful blue color. There were no waves in the water. It flowed peacefully along. She could see the bottom of the river. On the bottom there were twelve stones. On each of the stones were written the names of the twelve disciples. The stones were spaced out to where it looked like they formed a road in the river. There were fish swimming in the river, but they were not like she has ever seen. These fish were peaceful and swimming harmoniously together. There was a sign on the bank of the river. On the sign was written The River of Life. "So that is what took place at the park," Gabbi thought. When all those people got saved they drank from the river of life.

As she was admiring the river, Kathryn Kuhlman approached her. "Have you been waiting long?" Kathryn asked. "No, I just got here," Gabbi said. Kathryn had a huge smile on her face and said, "Oh the beauty of paying the price daughter." "What do you mean?" Gabbi asked. "The price you payed giving away two bicycles, paying for lunches, losing friends, and hanging out with the misfits of society paid off in the park. That little girl would not have received her healing if it were not for the price you paid. That precious couple would not be together if you did not pay the price. Those people were not at the park because it was such a nice day. They were sent there for you. God told me I am so pleased with Gabbi that I am going to reward her. She don't even know why she wants to go to the park because I have made special arrangements just for her. You see daughter, your spirit discerned the time and season for your next miracle. I am so happy for you," Kathryn said. "Why did you call me daughter?" Gabbi asked. "Why, I'm your spiritual mother Gabbi," Kathryn said. "I don't understand," Gabbi said. "In life you have a physical mother. She is a very beautiful mother Gabbi, inside and out. Don't ever mistreat her. You also have a spiritual mother. Sometimes a person has one that is still alive and well. Others have one in Heaven. You have a spiritual mother in Heaven. The mantle that was on me is on you," Kathryn said. Suddenly, there was a mantle in Kathryn's hands. She took the mantle and wrapped it around Gabbi's shoulders. "This mantle is my prophetic mantle. I give it to you. Your life will touch more than mine ever could. The price for this mantle is heavier than you have ever paid. You will pay the price and pass the test with flying colors. As you use the mantle it will multiply. Once it multiplies, God will tell you who to share it with. You will share it until it is time to pass it. Once God is ready for you to pass it on to the next generation, he will place someone in your life that will take the torch and run with it. Don't keep the mantle past its life cycle. You will live to pass the mantle on to the next generation," Kathryn said as she left Gabbi standing at the river.

Gabbi began following the river of life. She walked admiring the scenery. She noticed as she walked the trees seemed to take notice of her. There was one tree in particular that caught her attention. It was a large sycamore tree. The bark on this tree was a beautiful brown color. The bark did not look rough like trees on earth do. The bark on this tree had a velvet look. She reached out and touched the tree. The bark felt like her Elsa blanket. So soft and fluffy. How could this be? The leaves looked as if they were turning for Fall. They were a beautiful blood red. What caught Gabbi's attention about the leaves were their shape. These leaves were not a shape she would think of when she thought of leaves. The leaves she looks at have three finger looking shapes. These leaves were in the shape of a cross. Why did they look like that? "You must tell people about the price I paid for them on Calvary," Jesus spoke to her spirit. "This tree is placed here by the river of life to remind those that have gone on before you what their salvation cost me. As they look on this tree they rejoice because I paid the price allowing them into Heaven," Jesus said. "You must be hidden behind the cross. Not so you can be seen, but so I can be seen through you. Move on but always remember this tree. As you remember you must tell others what I did for them," Jesus concluded.

Gabbi continued on her journey. She went a little farther when she saw her Uncle Kenny. Kenny always had a smile on his face. As she approached him his smile broadened. "I want to share something with you Gabbi," Kenny said. "Okay Uncle Kenny. I love hearing your stories," Gabbi said. "When I was on earth I was close to your dad. No one else in the family was as close to him as I was. One time I decided to take him on the truck with me. Every Friday night I had to go from Marion Illinois to Fenton Missouri to deliver parts for Fabick. It was a lonely trip and I was tired of going by myself. I decided to take your dad. His face lit up every time we went in the truck. I gave him a CB handle. His name was Daffy Duck... "snicker", he loved that handle. As he grew up I moved away. I didn't get to see him as much. He does not know that I missed our times we spent together. The last time I saw him I took out a CB he gave me from the van he had. It got totaled and he thought of me when he was getting rid of the CB. I planned on coming back and seeing him again, but God had other plans. I died three days after his birthday. He takes this day hard. Tell him not to take it hard anymore, because just as I got to see him graduate from college, I too had a graduation day. One day he will see me again. Tell him to rejoice in knowing that," Kenny said.

After he shared this story with her he spent a few minutes with her. He was fishing when she walked up. Suddenly another pole appeared. He had Gabbi pick up the pole, and he taught her how to fish. You could tell he loved being a teacher, especially to members of his family. "I watch over your dad while he sleeps. I pray and ask God to help him in everyday life. Sometimes he can be quite wreck-less, so I ask God to guard his footsteps. I watch over you as well," Kenny said. Gabbi spent a while with Kenny before he got up to walk away. "Don't go," Gabbi said. "I must go now Gabbi, but don't worry, I will visit you often. When you get to Heaven we will be together forever. I will take you and your dad fishing often," Kenny said. "I love you Uncle Kenny," Gabbi said. "I love you too little Skinflint," Kenny said as he disappeared.

Suddenly, Jesus appeared with her grandma Mary. Gabbi did not have the chance to be around grandma much. They lived far away from her and did not get to come for a visit much. Grandma began to share with her about her dad growing up. How she took him in as a baby. She knew sometimes her dad didn't appreciate her for it. Gabbi could tell it bothered her grandma. She told Gabbi why she took her dad to church all of the time. She expressed the importance of serving God. There are many things in life a person can serve. Some serve their job. Some serve their family. Some put money as their god, but as her grandma explained, those things are going to fade away. Those things were going to cause a person to go to Hell. Serving God brings life. Serving God brings wholeness to your life. She urged Gabbi to put God first in every area of her life. She prompted her to love and respect her family always. As she got done she gave Gabbi a hug and walked off with Jesus.

Gabbi learned a lot from this short visit to Heaven. She was on a mission to reach the lost. Seeing and hearing from Kathryn, Kenny and grandma was the boost she needed to continue her journey in fulfilling her assignment.

CHAPTER 8
FULFILLING HER ASSIGNMENT

Gabbi could not wait to return to school. She learned a lot on this last trip to Heaven. She wanted to share this knowledge with others. If one person came to the Lord this trip was worth it. She remembered the other times she shared Jesus with people. She thought about Olivia and the experience she had with God. She was the first person she won to the Lord. She was sad because Olivia was not around anymore, and she did not know if she was serving the Lord today.

Her mind went to the day Melissa, Timmy, and Tommy came to the Lord. She smiled thinking about how Timmy was in Heaven today because he accepted the Lord before he died. As she was thinking about this Timmy appeared in her bedroom. "Gabbi, tell as many people you can how beautiful Heaven is. You have visited several times. I saw you the last time you visited when you was talking to your uncle. I live in Heaven, and it is worth all you go through on earth. I was not expecting to be in Heaven the day you led me to Jesus. That is the neat thing about all of this. I miss my mom and siblings, but to come back to earth, I never want to live there again. I am happy where I am, and you must tell people," Timmy said. With tears in her eyes Gabbi made him a promise she would share Jesus with others.

As he disappeared her mind went back to the day Joseph's life was changed. He had made great improvements in his life. He no longer has as many outbursts as he used to. Watching him get baptized was the best day of her life. He is serving the Lord today, and she helped. She was grateful God placed such an assignment over her life. She does not want to let him down.

All the bicycles she gave away. All the lunches she bought for other kids. All the times she was made fun of came down to this one moment in time. This was going to be the biggest thing she has faced in her life. All those she led to the Lord was a warm up. Now, she was going to go for the big harvest. She was going for the gusto, and she needed the Lord's help.

She got down on her knees and began to pray. "Oh God I accept the assignment you gave me. I must confess I am nervous. There are so many souls at school that need you. Help me reach them. Help me help them make this all important decision for you. I truly want to make a difference in people's life. Give me the right words to say, and the strength to say them. Help me have the courage to stand even when people make fun of me, Amen" Gabbi prayed. "I will not only help you, I will empower you," Jesus said.

As she got to school she ran across some of her friends. Suddenly, boldness rose up in her. She began sharing Jesus with them. Some of her friends walked away as she was talking, but this did not stop her. She kept sharing with those that stayed. She shared her last trip to Heaven. Told them about the sycamore tree she saw and what it represented. As she was talking her face began to shine. The kids standing there was in amazement as they saw her face glow. One of her friends asked her what she must do to be saved. Gabbi began to share with them the plan of salvation. As she did those around her prayed and God truly came into their lives. People passing by them stopped and began to pray because of the glory that was around Gabbi and her friends.

At lunch she bought three kids their lunches. As she paid for their lunch a door was opened for her to share Christ with them. As she shared with them the three kids and five others around them prayed and accepted Jesus. One of the kids at the table was suffering from ulcers. The kid noticed the pain in her stomach stopped as they were praying. Another kid had a leg shorter than the other one. The leg grew out in front of everyone around the table. When everyone standing around the table saw this, more kids prayed and asked God into their lives.

After lunch Gabbi was called into the office. The principal noticed how Gabbi was making a difference in the school. There was a pep rally scheduled for later that day. It was supposed to be a rally for the game that was taking place that night. The principal changed the rally and allowed Gabbi to share her faith. Gabbi agreed to do the pep rally.

At the pep rally the whole school was gathered in the gym. They audience was excited not only because of the rally, but because they were allowed out of class to attend. They loved every opportunity they had to miss being in class. Some of the kids were missing Math, and some were missing English, but all were in attendance and excited about being there. They erupted as the principal started the rally. They were expecting the cheerleaders to lead them in cheers as the basketball players took to the floor. They were not expecting to come in contact with a decision. This was not just any ordinary decision they were going to be confronted with. This decision was going to make the difference between Heaven and Hell. Suddenly, the principal had Gabbi come up to the stage.

The kids were shocked. Some cheered and some began to boo as she walked up to the stage. No matter what position they took, Their life was not going to be the same. She looked at her classmates sitting in the audience. Suddenly, boldness rose up in her. As she began to share Jesus with the crowd her countenance began to change. Some of the students reported Gabbi was glowing. Some reported she had the appearance of an angel. No matter what was reported, half of the student body made a decision for Christ. They rushed out of their seats and came to the stage and knelt. The other half of the student body chose to stay in their sins. While this hurt Gabbi, it did not deter her. There were five kids that got healed. God truly moved in that place.

The school was turned upside down by one girl that made the decision to go against the grain and stand for Jesus. It was amazing how one person to make a difference in so many lives, but Gabbi was that one person. She was a judge when needed, but mainly stood as a prophet. She found out you never know what God will do through a person if they are willing and obedient to be all he wants them to be. This school year was a school year like no other. This school year God reclaimed the school Gabbi attended for himself. While other schools may still be used by evil, Gabbi's school was transformed by the Lord. It would not have happened if there wasn't a girl that stood as the judge over sin, and the prophet for right. The world needs more kids like Gabbi who is willing to make a stand for Christ. Then we will see a world that is changed, and one that God can look at and be proud. To God be the glory.

FROM THE AUTHOR

We live in a world that needs to know Christ. While the events in this story is fictional, the message is very real. Jesus loves you. He loves us so much he came to earth as a babe. He was the perfect son of God that chose to come live in an imperfect world as the son of man. He did this to redeem mankind from sin.

You do not have to go to Hell. There is a way out, and his name is Jesus. *For God so lived the world that he gave his only begotten son; that whosoever believeth in him, shall not perish, but have ever lasting life.* John 3:16. Will you accept the free gift God left us. Will you allow Jesus into your heart? You will not know true life until you accept life. I pray as you read this book that you allow God to speak to your heart. May you not be the same by the time you finish reading this book.

In his love

Tracy Henderson (Jeremiah 29:11).

Don't miss out!

Visit the website below and you can sign up to receive emails whenever Tracy Henderson publishes a new book. There's no charge and no obligation.

https://books2read.com/r/B-A-XBQU-ADWGC

BOOKS 2 READ

Connecting independent readers to independent writers.

Also by Tracy Henderson

Family Mantle
Gabbi's Heavenly Visitation
The Judge and the Prophet

Inheritance Series
Inheritance by Fire

Standalone
Gabbi's Amazing Dream
`When I See the Blood

About the Author

As a child I was raised in church. I wasn't sent to church I was taken. I accepted my call to preach at seventeen years old, but something was missing. I had religion, but not relationship. In June of 2019 God gloriously saved me. It was an Apostle Paul like conversion. I was lying in bed on June 5, 2019 and developed chest pains and could not talk. Suddenly a bright light appeared to me, and I was taken out of my body. As I was taken up I heard the words "You have not delivered my message yet", and I was set back down. I was introduced to one of my spiritual fathers Apostle David E. Taylor in 2019, by a staff member. I wasn't quite sure he was for real until I had a vision about him and I in a hospital praying for people. He introduced me to spiritual inheritance through a book he wrote on it. Since then I have been on a quest to find the true meaning of spiritual inheritance. I pray not only through my ministry of preaching, but through my writing I am able to deliver God's message. I pray as people read my material their lives are changed as mine was. That will be my legacy I leave to the world.